P9-CCO-042

WITHDRAWN

First published in Switzerland under the title *Timo und Pico ziehen um.*

First published in the United States, Great Britain, Canada, Australia, and New Zealand in 2012 by NorthSouth Books Inc., an imprint of NordSüd Verlag AG, CH-8005 Zürich, Switzerland.

Distributed in the United States by NorthSouth Books Inc., New York 10016.
Library of Congress Cataloging-in-Publication Data is available.
Printed in Germany by Grafisches Centrum Cuno GmbH & Co. KG, 39240 Calbe, June 2012.
ISBN: 978-0-7358-4090-4
1 3 5 7 9 • 10 8 6 4 2

www.northsouth.com

Anke Wagner • Eva Eriksson

Tim's BIG Move!

NorthSouth
New York / London

Tim is very nervous.
He's moving to Calabash.

"It will be exciting," his parents tell him.
"It will be exciting," Tim tells Pico.
Pico is Tim's best cuddle buddy, and always has been.

But there's a problem.
Pico doesn't want to move.

He thinks Tim's room is very cozy.

Pico has a little house in the corner, with everything just so, exactly how he likes it.

"Don't worry, Pico, everything will be just fine," says Tim.

"In Calabash, the sun shines much more," says Tim.

Pico thinks, I don't like it if it's too hot.

"There will be lots of tall trees to climb," says Tim.

Pico thinks, I don't like the jungle either.

"And apart from all that, it's really close to the deep blue sea."

But I can't swim! thinks Pico in despair.

"We'll live in a big house," says Tim.

Pico thinks, How will I be able to climb the stairs?

"And best of all," says Tim happily, "we'll make lots of new friends."

Help! thinks Pico.

Pico is very pale. Pico is worried.
Tim and Pico, Pico and Tim.

No new friends, please!

He doesn't need anybody else.
Just Tim.
For ever and ever.

Tim wants to start packing right away.

Pico doesn't help; he wants to sit in the corner and think things over.
Pico is scared that Tim won't want him anymore when he has new friends.
Because his new friends are more interesting,

or more beautiful,

or stronger,

or braver,

or can swim.

Pico sits on the suitcase so that Tim can close it properly.

Pico feels better.

Tim is taking him along after all—and
holds him tight all the way to Calabash.

Finally they arrive.

Tim is very excited about his new home and everything else, too.

He helps his parents unpack.

Pico rests.

He looks all around; there are no new friends in sight.

What a relief.

Tim is tired out from working. He sleeps like a log and holds Pico tight.

Pico is very happy.

Next day they go out to explore.

The sun is shining brightly in the sky, not too hot, just right.

In the garden is a first-class climbing tree.

And in the house there are lots of nooks and crannies, great for playing in.

That afternoon Tim goes with his parents for a boat trip.

Still no new friends in sight,

thinks a relieved Pico.

Next day Tim goes to his new kindergarten.
Pico goes, too.

Help, so many children!

Pico starts to feel unwell.
These could be new friends.
He's worried about losing Tim.

Hey, what's Tim doing?

He's talking to a girl wearing pink overalls.
The girl is building a town.
Tim asks if he can play, too.

She says he can.
They're both laughing.
Having fun.

Pico is jealous.
Now the town is finished, and it looks great.

What's the girl doing?

She's going to get something.

Someone.

"This is Emma," says Hannah. Hannah is the girl's name.
"Emma is my best cuddle buddy."

Tim and Hannah show Pico and Emma the town.

It's great.

Just right for Pico and Emma.
They have lots of fun and don't want to go home.

KiNDER-
GARTEN

"What nice new friends we have," says Tim.
"What do you think, Pico?"

Pico is shocked. Tim is right.
Tim has a new friend, and Pico has one, too.

Four friends are just as good as two.

"But you," says Tim to Pico, and holds him very tightly, "are my best friend for ever and ever."
Pico smiles because it feels so wonderful.